Cranky Pants

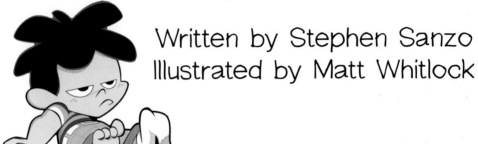

Written by Stephen Sanzo
Illustrated by Matt Whitlock

🐾 Cranky Pants Publishing

To my grammas
- S.S.

To Chad R.
- M.W.

Published by Cranky Pants Publishing, LLC, P.O. Box 1091, Arlington, MA 02474-0020
Cranky Pants Publishing is distributed to the trade by Biblio Distribution (a sister company of NBN)

ISBN 0-9759627-0-1
Library of Congress Control Number: 2004097325

Printed in the United States

First Edition
3 5 7 9 10 8 6 4 2

www.crankypantspublishing.com

I don't want to get up this morning.

Last night, I had scary dreams about a big, green, hairy monster...

and a mean, ugly, blue dog that ate my delicious peanut butter and jelly sandwich.

I don't want to get dressed...

and I can't tie my shoes.

My dad is in the kitchen making breakfast.

My sister is in her high chair yelling "cuckoo head!" at me.

I am still cranky.

It's raining out and I have to wear my rubbery, yellow raincoat.

I think my raincoat is made of cement.

I can't move my arms.

I am cranky and I don't even want to jump in the puddles...

or stick out my tongue to catch the rain...

or make chicken soup with mud water.

There is a lot of pushing in line at school.

I am in the middle getting mushed.

My teacher, Miss Dilly, has us sing songs to start the day.

I am cranky and I don't want to sing.

Today we are drawing pictures of
our favorite things.

Some kids are
making dinosaurs...

and ice cream...

and one girl
drew a big, fat
cat.

I can't think of what
to draw.

I am still cranky.

Lunch today is grilled cheese sandwiches.

I love grilled cheese.

I should have drawn a picture of a grilled cheese sandwich.

But, I am cranky
and not very hungry.

We play kickball in
the afternoon.

I am in left field looking at the clouds.

My mom picks me up after school.

Miss Dilly tells her I was a
cranky pants today.

My mom has just come back from a
work trip. She tells me all about it in
the car.

She is a doctor at the zoo.

She had to go to another zoo to help a big gorilla with a tummy ache.

I like my mom's stories.

I am getting hungry.

I feel less cranky.

When we get home my sister is asleep.

My dad bought us pepperoni pizza!

My dad and mom are happy to see each other and they talk a lot.

I am just happy eating my pizza.

I go upstairs and get ready for bed.

I have no trouble getting my PJs on.

I am nice and cozy under my blanket.

My mom and dad read my favorite story.

When the story is done, my mom kisses me on the cheek.

My silly dad puts the covers over my head like he always does.

I am smiling when
they turn off the light.

I close my eyes...

I am not cranky anymore.